THE MAD MISSION OF JASMIN J.

published by Hodder Children's Books:

The Deadly Secret of Dorothy W.

JON BLAKE

THE MAD MISSION OF JASMIN J.

ILLUSTRATED BY KORKY PAUL

*Hodder
Children's
Books*

A division of Hodder Headline Limited

Chapter One

Six months had gone by since that fantastic night, and life was becoming unbearable. When you have *such* a fantastic night, ordinary things like painting your toenails and watching *Top Of The Pops* suddenly lose their appeal. You want more fantastic nights, you *need* them, and one way or another, you've got to get them.

So what was this fantastic night? Well, it was the night that I won the Toxico Children's Book award with my novel *The Ghost of the Chocolate Dinosaur*. It was the greatest book ever written, and I alone wrote it. With my kind-of-friend Kevin Shilling. And a twelve-foot man-eating monster called Mr Collins. I can't be bothered to explain all that. Just read *The Deadly Secret of Dorothy W.* by Mr Jon Blake. He got quite a few things wrong, but at least he tried.

Anyway, after this great night, Kevin and I decided to write a follow-up. As usual, Kevin got the ideas (millions of them), and I sorted out the good ones from the rubbish – except the good ones were few and far between. Winning the Toxico had severely affected Kevin's head, which wasn't that healthy to start with.

The danger signs were there in the first days after the award, when we were doing endless interviews with papers and magazines and radio stations. To quote one example:

X-MAG: How do you think success will affect you?

KEVIN: How will success affect Kevin Shilling? Well, Kevin's a pretty level-headed guy. He'll get on with life, same as before, I guess. The only real difference is he won't have to hang around with losers.

To be fair, Kevin didn't actually dump any of his old mates once he became famous. He didn't have to, because he had no old mates to dump. He got quite a few new friends though. Both of us did. They were friends who kept telling us how great we were then asking if they could borrow a tenner. I would have showed them all the door, but Kevin was happy to keep them around. He never lent them a tenner though, so after a while they stopped coming.

The book publishers stopped coming too. When *Chocolate Dinosaur* sold a million and was translated into Chinese, Japanese, Punjabi and Scouse, everyone was fighting for our next book.

But the sad fact was, we'd only written *Chocolate Dinosaur* with the help of Mr Collins, and Mr Collins was no longer around. He'd escaped from the Dorothy Wordsearch School for Gifted Young Writers and hadn't been seen since, although some kids reckoned they'd seen him hanging on the back of a train heading for the Channel Tunnel.

Everyone wanted us to write at least a hundred pages, but without Mr Collins, we couldn't quite get that far. Our best effort was six and a half. Kevin suggested changing the typeface to seventy-two point, so all the words looked like

this

but somehow I didn't think the publishers would fall for that.

So that was the situation one Easter holiday morning as we sat in our deluxe garden shed going through the mail. Or, to be more accurate, *I* sat, while Kevin walked backwards round the room at a hundred miles an hour. He'd been eating cherry jelly rings again. I'd *told* Kevin not to eat cherry jelly rings, because they made him totally hyper, sure to do anybody's head in, especially mine.

As usual, there were a few fan letters in the mail, plus a couple of letters asking if we'd like to give money to something-or-other. But there was also an envelope marked Little Angel Publishing Inc.

"Kevin!" I said. "It's a letter about *Major Plopdrop*!"

Major Plopdrop was Kevin's latest great idea. It was one of the funniest things ever written – according to Kevin. Something had gone very wrong in Kevin's potty training, and as a result anything to do with toilets turned him into a laughing hyena. Personally, I thought that toilets were useful things, necessary even, but not especially hilarious, even if they were to get up and do a song and dance.

Opening the letter, I soon realized that the editor at Little Angel Publishing shared my view:

Dear Kevin and Jasmin,

Thank you for sending me your manuscript 'Major Plopdrop'. I thought you set the scene very well in the opening paragraphs and I particularly enjoyed the description of Captain Paperwork.

Unfortunately the rest of the story was pants.

The best of luck in finding another publisher for your story.

Yours regretfully,
Primrose Handwash
Junior Editor, Little Angel Publishing

Kevin read my expression. He'd seen it fifty times before.

"Don't tell me," he said. "Another put-down."

"They did say some nice things about it," I replied.

"They always do that," complained Kevin.

"I did say it wasn't funny," I said.

"Who cares what you think?" warbled Kevin. He tipped back his head, let out a savage yowl, then started bouncing round the room, nutting the walls.

When I bought the shed, I thought it would be a lovely peaceful place to work in. I did it out with colourful rag rugs, Winnie-the-Pooh beanbags and comfy armchairs. I put wooden blinds up at the windows to stop my four brothers and sisters making faces.

But no matter how peaceful I made it, Kevin's head still turned it into a war zone.

I was rapidly reaching the stage where I would have to say That's Enough. Forget fame. Forget fortune. Give me my old life back again – a life where I only saw Kevin in class and, if I made a little wall with my books, didn't see him at all.

"Kevin," I pleaded. "We've got to write something else. We made an agreement. Five hundred words a day on weekends."

"What's the point," muttered Kevin, thumping a beanbag. "No one wants it."

I took a deep breath, switched off the PC, and turned to face him. "OK," I said. "You want to give up, let's give up."

"Bye then," said Kevin, and walked out, just like that.

Good riddance, I said to myself. If Kevin thought I was running after him, he had another think coming. I would just sit here and feel really sorry for myself, so sorry it would almost be pleasant.

Unfortunately, Mum had other plans

for me. She appeared at the blinds, holding an imaginary telephone to her ear and mouthing frantically, "Phone!"

I answered the call, expecting the usual message from Gaynor, or Josie, or Cath, telling me how bored they were. But it was a grown-up voice on the phone – posh, but eager and friendly.

"Jasmin!" it said. "I'm so pleased to talk to you!"

"Do I know you?" I asked.

"I'm Lottie Popsock from Peebo Press. I'm sure you've heard of us. We publish the world-famous Fluffy Bunny Button series."

At the mention of Fluffy Bunny Button, my blood chilled. Fluffy Bunny Button was, of course, the pitiful creation of Dorothy Wordsearch, probably the worst children's author in history. You'll remember her from *The Deadly Secret of Dorothy W.*, unless you *still* haven't read it, despite me just telling you to.

"As you know, Dorothy Wordsearch has sadly passed away," continued Lottie Popsock.

"Yes," I said, trying to sound sorry. "I was there when Mr Collins ate her."

"Terrible business," said Lottie Popsock.

"Frightful," I agreed.

"And the saddest thing of all," said Lottie Popsock, "is that Fluffy Bunny Button has just gone supersonic in Taiwan."

"It has?" I replied, doubtfully.

"Children in Taiwan can't get enough of him," trilled Lottie Popsock.

I made a mental note never to visit Taiwan, wherever it was.

"The problem is," continued Lottie Popsock, "since Dorothy is no more, there are no more Fluffy Bunny Buttons in the pipeline. The only solution … is to get someone else to write them."

There was a long pause. I sensed that Lottie was gearing herself up to ask me something, but I couldn't think what that thing might be. Unless …

… no …

… not that …

"So," she continued, "we were *wondering* if you and *Kevin*—"

I was in like a flash. "Let me stop you right there," I interrupted. "I know Kevin and I are only kids, but we're serious artists, see, and we write quality stories, see, whereas Fluffy Bunny Button is like the *saddest*, most *pathetic* character in the whole history of books, and the very thought of his stupid, doe-eyed face makes me want to throw up my breakfast!"

"Oh," said Lottie Popsock, shocked.

"Sorry," I added.

"So am I," replied Lottie Popsock. "We were going to offer you fifty thousand pounds."

There was another brief pause, while I picked myself up off the floor.

"How much?" I asked.

"Fifty thousand pounds," repeated Lottie.

"For *one book*?"

"Yes, but obviously we'll be looking for sequels. If the first book goes well, we may be able to offer rather more for the rest. And, of course, we'll pay for the flights to Taiwan so you can do personal appearances. Still, if you're not interested …"

"Did I *say* I wasn't interested?" I replied.

Chapter Two

I said I wasn't running after Kevin, and I didn't. I went on my bike. I caught him up by the waste tip, he told me not to bother, I mentioned the fifty grand, and five minutes later we were back in the shed.

Once the excitement had died down, however, we began to realize the job wasn't that easy. We couldn't just write any old rubbish. We had to write rubbish that sounded like the rubbish Dorothy Wordsearch wrote. We'd heard a few extracts from the books, but we'd never actually read one.

"What we need to do," I said, "is to read the lot."

"Get lost!" sneered Kevin.

"No, seriously!" I protested. "That's how Mr Collins made *The Ghost of the Chocolate Dinosaur*. He swallowed hundreds of stories and then it just came."

Kevin still wasn't keen. Reading thirty-nine books would mean sitting still for well over five minutes, which was Kevin's absolute limit.

"Maybe look at *one*," he mumbled.

"No, Kevin," I replied. "We need to know everything about him. We need to know what he looks like. We need to know how he behaves. We need to know all the other characters. We need to know where they all live, and what kind of adventures they have. In short, Kevin, we need to *think like Dorothy Wordsearch*."

The moment I said this, a terrible

sinking feeling came over me. Kevin was also looking anxious.

"Do you think this is a good idea?" I asked.

Kevin eyes flitted from side to side. "We need the money," he gabbled.

"That's it," I agreed. "We need the money."

I don't know how many books Kevin read in the end. He *said* sixteen, but when I quizzed him he could only remember the plots of two, and not very well at that. Meanwhile I'd got through eleven, reminding myself again and again what Mrs Frizzell, our local librarian, always told us: reading is good for you. Any reading. Even this.

All the while, however, I was haunted by a terrible thought: maybe I really would start thinking like Dorothy Wordsearch – maybe I'd actually turn into her! One day soon, I would find myself shopping for a paisley shawl. Words like *splendid* would slip into my conversation. I'd talk down to people in a little sing-song voice, and buy a house called The Old Vicarage, and, last but not least, marry a man called Winston.

Still, as Kevin said, we did need the money.

And we *could* stop after writing one book.

Writing that book, however, would not be as easy as I first thought. Dorothy Wordsearch had used up just about every corny idea going, and even Kevin's manic imagination couldn't seem to come up with a new one.

"I know," I suggested, towards the end of a fruitless afternoon in the shed, "let's just buy him a new toy."

"But he's *always* getting new toys," complained Kevin. "*Fluffy Bunny Button's Brand New Bow-tie … Fluffy Bunny Button's Super Christmas Train Set …*"

"Yes, but this will be something different … like a football … or a bike!"

"Oh, not a bike!" moaned Kevin.

"What's wrong with a bike?" I protested.

"Motorbike then," suggested Kevin. "1200cc Harley Chopper."

"Oh sure," I scoffed. "Why not make him a Hell's Angel?"

"Yeah," said Kevin. "With leathers, and a helmet, and a death's head belt buckle."

It wasn't going to be easy to agree anything with Kevin. I patiently explained why Fluffy Bunny Button wouldn't have a 1200cc chopper and a death's head belt buckle, but his mind was set on it. After a long and exhausting argument, we finally made a truce: Fluffy Bunny Button would get a bike, *not* a motorbike, but he could still wear *some* of the gear.

"I'm giving him a full-face helmet," said Kevin. "Like Robocop."

"A full-face helmet?" I sneered. "What's he going to do with his ears?"

"Tie them round his head," replied Kevin.

"Then he'll be blindfolded!" I scoffed.

"Not round the front, stupid!" cried Kevin. "Round the back!"

I still couldn't see it, but there was no time for more arguments. I switched on the PC, and at last we began to write the story. In a weird way it was fun. The preparation had really paid off, and it was just like turning on a tap. Words flowed like water, or, to be more accurate, like sewage, since that was what we were writing.

Two sessions later, we had more than half the story. Fluffy Bunny Button had been given his bike, almost had an accident, and gone out and bought a helmet. Now we just needed a good ending. Kevin claimed he'd already got one in his head, but he wanted it to be a surprise for me. I didn't much like the sound of this. But Kevin insisted on taking the story home with him to finish off himself, and I didn't want to hold him back.

Next day Kevin came in looking well pleased with himself. He had finished the story, it was totally brilliant, and I would kill myself laughing when I saw it.

Anxiously, I read the first sentences Kevin had added:

That night, Fluffy Bunny Button left his lovely full-face helmet in the cupboard under the stairs. It was time for bee-bo beddy-byes.

Out crept Maggoty May the rat. "Ooh," he said, spying the lovely blue helmet. "That looks like a nice place to curl up." He crawled into the helmet and was soon sound asleep.

Next morning, when Fluffy Bunny Button put on his lovely helmet, he didn't notice Maggoty May inside it.

"What's that tickling?" he wondered. Then he saw his super new bike and forgot all about it.

Maggoty May was starting to panic. There was no way out. And when a rat is trapped, he has only one instinct – to dig.

I put down the story. "Is this going where I think it's going?" I asked.

"It's brilliant!" said Kevin. "Just read it!"

Warily, I read on. But not for long. The rest of the story was even sicker than I'd feared. "Kevin," I said, gravely. "You really worry me."

Kevin laughed.

"Little children have got to read this!" I protested.

Kevin laughed again.

"No one's going to publish it," I said.

Suddenly Kevin looked offended. "Why not?" he asked.

"It'll give children nightmares!"

"It'll make 'em laugh!"

There really was no point in trying to reason with Kevin. Kevin was not a reasonable person. Most of the time his head was so full of noise and nonsense, he didn't hear me at all.

The only answer was to finish the story myself – except, as you may know, I was never much of an ideas person, unless I was about to be eaten by a twelve-foot monster. To my surprise, however, once I stopped relying on Kevin and put my own mind to the job, ideas did come. Really rubbishy ideas, just like Dorothy Wordsearch would have. They were perfect.

Within a day I had finished *Fluffy Bunny Button's Brand New Bike*, and sent it off to Lottie Popsock, without ever telling Kevin I'd changed his ending.

Three days later I got an e-mail saying that Lottie Popsock was delighted with the story.

Chapter Three

That, then, was how Kevin and I came to be on the train to London one bright nearly-spring day, under a yellow sun and candyfloss clouds. It was almost like one of the pictures in the Fluffy Bunny Button books, and that gave me a kind of secure, cosy, warm feeling. Not that I was starting to *like* the books … but there was no harm in liking the pictures, was there?

Kevin was quiet for once, chewing through a huge selection of jelly sweets and probably imagining his own pictures. Blue sky, green trees, waving cornfields, and a filthy great rat crawling out of Fluffy Bunny Button's eye socket.

Except, of course, that bit wasn't in the story any more.

We eventually arrived at St Pancras and walked through London like we owned it. Lottie Popsock was there to greet us at the doorway of Peebo House. She had wild blonde curls and a big bright smile, but the moment our eyes met I could tell something was wrong.

Lottie Popsock took us up to her office, gave us orange squash and custard creams, then turned to the subject of *Fluffy Bunny Button's Brand New Bike*.

"I thought it was a marvellous story," she said, "especially the ending, where Fluffy Bunny Button gives the tooth fairy a ride home in his basket."

A look of total bewilderment came over Kevin, while I smiled sweetly.

"We were just about to give you a

contract …" said Lottie Popsock. Her voice trailed off and she looked down at the floor.

"But?" I asked.

Lottie Popsock searched for words. "Something rather extraordinary has happened," she said.

With an apologetic smile, she reached into her top drawer and drew out a script, carefully prepared in a plastic cover. "This arrived in the post this morning," she added.

I read the title on the cover:

Fluffy Bunny Button's Fabulous Hit Record
A new Fluffy Bunny Button adventure
By Dorothy Wordsearch

"But … that's impossible," I blurted.

"At first we thought someone had dug out an old unpublished story," said Lottie Popsock, "but it's dated this month."

"Maybe it's a forgery," I suggested.

"We checked the postmark," replied Lottie Popsock. "Lower Uppingham. That's where she lived … lives, rather."

"But I saw her being eaten!" I protested. "Every bit of her."

"It certainly is a mystery," said Lottie Popsock.

"Kevin," I said, "you saw Mr Collins eat her, didn't you?"

Kevin looked at me with a sullen glare. "You wrote out Maggoty May," he growled.

"I'm sorry?" said Lottie Popsock.

"Ignore him," I suggested.

"Whatever has happened," said Lottie Popsock, "we have to publish this book and not yours, I'm afraid."

I was gutted. Lottie Popsock tried to make it up to us by telling us how wonderful we were, but we'd heard all that before. We left the building in a cloud of depression which looked nothing like candyfloss.

"How could this happen?" I groaned.

"It's cos you wrote out Maggoty May," moaned Kevin.

"Oh, for goodness' sake, shut up about Maggoty May!" I cried. "If it wasn't for me, we wouldn't be here in the first place!"

"Oh yeah," grunted Kevin, "you're such a genius, Jasmin! Any ideas what to do now, Brain of Britain?"

Kevin had a really sarcastic look on his face, and I was determined to wipe it off. "Yeah, I've got an idea," I said.

"Come on then, Einstein."

"We go back to Dorothy Wordsearch's school ... and we find out what the hell is going on."

A look of dread came over Kevin's face. I smiled coolly, hiding the utter terror I was also feeling.

Chapter Four

We left for Lower Uppingham three days later. Mum was a bit iffy about me going back to the Dorothy Wordsearch school, especially as it was closed down, but I came up with a brilliant excuse. I'd love to tell you what it was, but unfortunately I can't, as you might try to use it yourself.

> **REMEMBER: VISITING HOUSES INHABITED BY THE LIVING DEAD IN THE MIDDLE OF NOWHERE IS DANGEROUS. DO NOT ATTEMPT TO IMITATE.**

I tried to be well-prepared. I packed a torch, a dictaphone, a polaroid camera and three packets of cherry jelly rings (you'll soon find out why). I know I *should* have packed a mobile, but I'd just had mine nicked, and I was sure Kevin would have one, except it turned out all six of his had been nicked. At least I was spared the ten thousand different answering tones he usually played.

We arrived at the nearest train station, which was T— (again it is not safe for me to give the precise details) and hired a taxi to the village. We didn't go straight to the old school as we wanted to ask a few questions of the locals first. If Dotty (as we called her) was still alive, she would surely have visited the shops at some time.

The post office seemed a good place to start. That was where she would have posted her story. It was a quaint little building of yellow brick, with postcards

in the window offering GARDENING
SERVICES, CHILD-MINDING, and
UNIQUE HAND-MADE POTTERY
VOLES.

A tall, stooping man stood behind the
counter, with a sad, vacant look on his
face. "Excuse me," I asked him, "we're
members of the Twitchy Tail Club and we
are looking for the famous children's
author Dorothy Wordsearch."

The tall sad man narrowed his eyes.
"You're not from round here, are you?"
he said.

"No," I replied.

"Thank goodness," added Kevin.

"If you had been from round here," said
the tall sad man, "you'd have been to the
service."

"Service?" I enquired.

The tall sad man indicated a faded
poster on the wall, which up to now we
hadn't noticed:

MEMORIAL SERVICE
FOR THE LATE DOROTHY WORDSEARCH
HER FAVOURITE HYMNS
READINGS FROM 'FLUFFY BUNNY BUTTON'
EXHIBITION OF SHAWLS

St Agnes Church, Sunday 1st September, 6 p.m.

"Dead, see," said the man. "Never did find the body, mind."

"Mmm," I replied. "So she hasn't posted anything here recently."

"Not recently, no," said the man, "being dead, like."

"So what's happened to her school?" I asked.

"All boarded up," replied the man. "Not a soul there now."

"Aha," I said. "Any questions you want to ask?" I asked Kevin.
Kevin thought for a few moments. "Do you sell sweets?" he said.

The taxi driver wasn't too happy about taking us to the old school. Since it had been boarded up, there were all kinds of rumours. The usual stuff – strange noises in the night, eerie glowing lights, dark shadowy figures. It didn't faze me of course, but Kevin went strangely quiet as we approached the gates. Climbing out of the taxi, he told me he had a confession.

"There's something you ought to know about me," he said.

"Go on," I replied, wearily.

"I was brought up by monkeys," said Kevin.

I checked my watch. "Hmm," I said. "If we make a quick tour, we should be back before dark."

"Did you hear what I just said?" bleated Kevin.

"Yes," I replied. "Have you got the torch?"

"I'm serious!" cried Kevin. "I was very small. My mum and dad were fighting, so I ran away, and monkeys found me and took me as one of their own. Didn't you notice there was something different about me?"

"Oh, yes," I replied. "I noticed that."

"One day," said Kevin, very seriously, "they will come for me again."

I let out a long sigh. "Kevin," I said, "why are you telling me this now?"

"I think the day is coming," replied Kevin.

"Oh, yes," I said. "And why is that?"

"I can sense it," replied Kevin. "Animal instinct."

"Not because you don't want to go into the old school?" I asked.

"I'll climb this tree," said Kevin, indicating a nearby oak. "That way I can keep a lookout on the school, and for the monkeys at the same time."

I began to object, but before I had got

three words out, Kevin was shinning up the tree. To my amazement, he really was a fantastically good climber. Come to think of it, with a bit more hair around his face …

Stop it right there, I told myself. This mission was dangerous enough as it was, without getting drawn into Kevin's fantasy world.

"OK," I said. "I'll go on without you. But don't forget I've got the cherry jelly rings."

I opened the gate and set off up the drive. It wasn't long before Kevin's footsteps were pattering anxiously after me. I had discovered long ago that controlling the sweet supply gave me almost complete mastery over Kevin. Fame and fortune had not changed that.

We passed the front lawn where Mr Collins gave birth to *The Ghost of the Chocolate Dinosaur*. No sign of him now, thank goodness, or of anyone else for that matter. Ahead of us, the old school was dark, deserted and not exactly inviting. Dreadful memories came washing over me, but at the same time, my heart was pumping with excitement and fascination. I felt I wasn't controlling my own hand as it reached out for the door handle.

Locked, of course.

"That's it," said Kevin. "Let's go."

"Wait right there," I ordered.

I looked around for another way in. All the downstairs windows were boarded up. On the first floor, however, the windows were still uncovered – and the top half of one was open!

"That's where you can get in!" I said.

"I can't get up there!" cried Kevin.

"Course you can!" I said. "You were brought up by monkeys."

"Did I say monkeys?" replied Kevin. "I meant rabbits."

"Kevin," I said. "I've just *seen* you climb.

Now get up on my shoulders, go up the rose trellis and get through that window!"

Kevin stood firm. I took out a cherry jelly ring.

"Want one?" I asked.

Kevin's mouth began to twitch.

"Before, not after," he replied.

I handed Kevin the prized sweet. I don't think he actually chewed it before he swallowed. Within seconds, it seemed, he was jittering up and down and mumbling rubbish to himself. I got down on one knee and he scrambled his way up to my shoulders. He weighed lighter than a feather but stank like goodness knows what.

"What's that disgusting smell?" I asked, staggering up to my full height.

"Think I stepped in something down the drive," replied Kevin.

"Thanks for telling me!" I spluttered.

"Any time," said Kevin.

The weight eased as Kevin caught hold of the rose trellis and began clambering up to the window. Once up on the ledge, the rest was easy.

Now all I had to do was wait, and hope Kevin did nothing too stupid.

A couple of minutes went by. Then, from deep inside the house, there was a muffled yell of horror. My stomach flipped. I heard Kevin's voice: "No! No! Get back!"

Chapter Five

"Kevin!" I bawled, hammering at the door.

A bolt loosened. Suddenly the door swung open. There was Kevin, completely alone, grinning stupidly and giving me a little wave.

"Kevin, you idiot!" I cried.

"Fooled you," said Kevin.

"What if someone heard?"

"There's no one here!"

"We don't know that!"

I stepped inside. The place certainly looked abandoned. But there was still that old school smell, of antiseptic, rubber mats and distant sponge pudding. In the dim light there was no sign of any furniture or pictures. The inside doors also seemed to be missing. I remembered that Mr Collins had smashed a couple on his rampage through the building, but certainly not all of them.

We wandered down to our old classroom. That too was empty, and seemed much bigger without desks and chairs – or Dotty, for that matter. Something else was different – the ceiling. I'd spent hours looking at the plaster mouldings up there while I was stuck for ideas. Now there were no plaster mouldings. The whole of the ceiling was covered in a wire mesh. I'd seen something like it before, but I couldn't remember where.

At this point Kevin turned on the light and went spinning round the empty room like demented frisbee. I noticed that the walls were covered in gouges and what looked like dark scorch marks – all about half a metre off the ground. I was just pondering on this when a more urgent thought struck me.

"The light's on!" I blurted.

"I switched it on, stupid!" said Kevin.

"But that means there's electricity," I replied.

"So?" said Kevin.

"So someone's living here!" I hissed.

Kevin stopped spinning. "Oh yeah," he mumbled.

I quickly flicked off the light. From now on we were speaking in whispers and taking it very slowly – not an easy task if you are Kevin Shilling.

Kevin was all for investigating the Secret Garden next. That, of course, was the place where Dotty had kept the monstrous Mr Collins. The last time I'd been there, I'd been struggling for my life, and I really wasn't keen to repeat the experience. I preferred to find out what had become of the room under the stairs – home of the wizened yet strangely powerful housekeeper, Miss Birdshot.

There had been big changes here as well. The little door had been changed to a metal grille, twice the width of the old opening and extremely secure. That hadn't been done without a reason.

"We need to get in there," I whispered.

Kevin gave a snort, as if to say Some Hope. It was increasingly clear that someone was using the old school for *something*, and that someone didn't want other someones to find out what that something was.

The old study was also locked. That was where Dotty had kept her pictures of her beloved late husband, Winston, the strange inventor who had made Mr Collins. I could tell you a lot more about Winston, but by now you *must* have read *The Deadly Secret of Dorothy W.*, so I won't bother.

We pressed on, upstairs. All the tiny prison-cell bedrooms were locked. But at the far end of the corridor, through some doors we'd never been allowed through, we found a whole lot more rooms, including one marked FACTORY. That was an odd name for a room, I thought. I approached this room cautiously, and as I did, became aware of a noise – a faint, soft, rattling noise.

The closer we got to the door, the louder it became.

"There's someone in there!" I hissed.

We held our breaths and listened harder. That was when it became clear to me. It was the sound of fingers rapping away at a keyboard.

"I'm going," said Kevin.

"No!" I whispered. "We've got to find out who it is!"

"Don't open the door!" hissed Kevin.

"I'm not going to open the door!" I replied.

"Then how do we find out?"

"We hide, then we wait for them to come out."

"What, all night?"

For once Kevin had a point. Whatever it was in there, it was going like the clappers and might carry on for hours. We didn't want to get stuck here for the night.

But there was another possibility. Part of the roof of the old school was flat, and it was just possible we could get across it and see into the study through a window.

We found a window which led on to the roof, pushed it open, and clambered out. By now the dusk was gathering, and the last of the birds were leaving the front lawn for their nests. We tiptoed over the slabs, drawn towards the one window which gave off light – an eerie, dim blue light.

"You look," said Kevin.

I took a deep breath and edged up beside the window. Just one glance, I told myself. Just one super-fast glance, and hope that whatever-it-was isn't looking out at the same time.

But what if they were? The risks were huge.

At this point I had another brainwave. My polaroid camera was still in my bag. I pulled it out of its case, held it for a millisecond in front of the window, and took a picture. Then I ran like a rabbit, with Kevin in hot pursuit. We scrambled back into the house.

"Let's get out of here now," I gasped.

We hurried down the stairs and along the hall towards the front door. But just at that second, to our absolute horror … the handle on the door began to turn.

"Quick!" I said. "The kitchen!"

I don't know why I opted for the

kitchen, except it wasn't far away and was full of cupboards. Most were too small to hide in, but my eyes fell on a larger door in the corner. Luckily it was open. We flung ourselves inside, into a cold, dark space not much bigger than a wardrobe. I was uncomfortably close to Kevin's sweaty armpit, but right at that moment, I didn't particularly care.

From the hallway came a deep, loud, blood-curdling laugh. Then another, except higher. There were crashes and yells and falling-about noises. A man (or a very husky woman) started raving at the top of his/her voice in a strange foreign language. Then I realized they were actually speaking English, a very slurred kind of English, the kind of English spoken by people when they have drunk twelve pints of lager.

"They're drunk!" I whispered.

"Ha!" said Kevin.

I felt kind of superior now, but not one

bit safer. There was no obvious way out of the hole we were in, unless maybe the drunken people collapsed and fell asleep, which didn't seem at all likely at that moment.

By now my eyes were adjusting to the dark. I realized we were in some kind of pantry. The shelves in front of us were stacked with rows and rows of flat red and green boxes – pizza boxes. There were at least fifty of them, and, as we soon discovered, they were not empty. Kevin crammed a fat mouthful of deep pan meat feast into his gob, but at that moment, we heard footsteps coming our way.

"Oh no!" I hissed. "They're coming for food!"

I looked around in desperation – and there, right next to our feet, was a trapdoor. I'd never realized the old school had a cellar, and Dotty had certainly never mentioned it. I vaguely realized we could be in for even bigger trouble down there, but there was little time to think. We hauled open the door, climbed down into the jet-black hole, and lowered the great block of wood back into place.

The smell was appalling – an odour of mushrooms, wet coal, stale dirty washing and open sewers. Something dripped on my head, and I jerked my face straight into a clinging cobweb, which went right over my eyes, up my nose and into my mouth. Somehow I stifled a scream, which was just as well, because up above there were footsteps in the pantry.

"*Something brushed against me!*" squeaked Kevin.

"What was it?" I quivered.

"Big … hairy … like a … *giant spider*!"

Kevin started flailing like a maniac, but all he hit was me. "Stop it!" I hissed, searching frantically through my bag for my pen torch.

I switched on the thin light. There were tears in Kevin's eyes. Not far away was a battered old plastic Christmas tree.

"*There's* your spider, you idiot!" I whispered.

I played the torch round the cellar. It truly was a dismal place. Some of the junk down there looked Victorian – metal buckets, a mangle, even a brown leather football. But that was not what really disturbed me. What really disturbed me was the bed at the far end, made of old tomato boxes, the bare bedside light-bulb, the camping gas stove and the tin saucepan full of mouldering food.

Someone had been living in this room.

And there was more. The walls were covered in writing and strange, obscure diagrams, carved out with bad charcoal or maybe just burnt sticks. It reminded me of a museum I once visited which had been a prison for soldiers of

Napoleon's army (or something like that).

"What *is* this place?" I asked out loud.

"Dunno," mumbled Kevin. "But thanks to you, we're stuck here."

"Ah well," I said. "Least things can't get any worse."

Kevin tried the bedside light. To my amazement, it worked, though it didn't give off much more light than my torch. I put the torch away, and as I did so, came upon my camera. In all the excitement, I'd clean forgotten the photo I'd taken. I detached it from the camera and held it beneath the light. Being a polaroid, I would have to pull the cover off it, then watch it develop. It was a bit like pulling a plaster off a wound, not knowing what grisly secret would be revealed.

With a trembly hand, I ripped back the cover. Slowly but surely, there before us, appeared the unmistakable features of the late Dorothy Wordsearch.

Chapter Six

As I have said before, there was no doubt that Dorothy Wordsearch had died. I had seen her disappear into Mr Collins's lethal cakehole, and heard the fearsome teeth chewing her like a boiled sweet. I know that surgeons can sometimes sew a finger back on, or even an arm, but there was no way they could turn a tin of minced beef back into a cow.

I stared again at the photo. Admittedly, you could only see the head and shoulders beside the computer, but there was absolutely no doubt who they belonged to.

The same hair, the same eyes – even the same paisley shawl.

"M-maybe it's an identical twin," suggested Kevin.

"With an identical mole on her chin?" I scoffed. "I don't think so!"

"Then she must be a … a zombie."

My toes curled. The word "zombie" had never sounded more sinister, or more real. I stared again at the photo, and noticed that the eyes were strangely glassy … dead, even.

"I'm going home," said Kevin.

"But if we can prove Dorothy Wordsearch is a zombie," I replied, "Lottie won't publish her book."

"Why not?" asked Kevin.

"Of course she won't!" I protested. "How can she do book signings if she's a zombie? How can she visit libraries? The whole point about Fluffy Bunny Button is he's *nice*, and *cuddly*, and *safe*.

Kids think he's written by a kindly old aunty, not the walking dead."

"*I'd* buy a book if it was written by the living dead," said Kevin.

"Yeah, well, you're weird," I replied.

At this point a strange commotion began above our heads. It sounded like someone was mowing the lawn, except at fifty miles an hour, and indoors. There were more whoops and cries and loud, manic laughter. The noise seemed to be moving round the house, very fast. Every so often there was a loud THUMP as if someone was hitting the wall with a rubber mallet.

The fun and games went on and on, until my eyes became heavy, and I drifted off to the sound of Kevin hungrily munching pizza.

When I woke it was morning, and Kevin had disappeared. His bag was also gone, and he'd thoughtfully left the trap door wide open. Upstairs the noise had stopped. Cursing my so-called friend, I made plans for my own escape. There was no way I was conducting this investigation on my own.

They'd certainly been in the pantry. Half the pizzas had gone, and a few empty boxes were strewn about. I peered through the door, to see the kitchen silent and empty.

So far, so good. On feather toes I crept towards the hallway. It was only a short dash down there to the front door. But as I glanced through the doorway I was shocked to see Kevin, down on his knees, tugging at the bottom of the front door.

"You!" I gasped.

Kevin looked up, but didn't seem embarrassed, just purple with effort. "Can't get the bolt undone!" he hissed.

I hurried to join him. "What did you think you were doing, leaving without me?" I snarled.

"I was coming back for you," said Kevin. "Honest."

"Sure," I replied. "Here, let me have a go!"

I got down to the floor and the two of us yanked away at the stuck bolt.

It was at this point that a large, heavy hand landed on my shoulder.

"Can I help at all?" asked a deep, sing-song voice.

I leapt back. There above me was the strangest man I'd ever seen. His hands and neck were all wrinkly like a sixty-year-old, but his face was stretched taut like a blown-up balloon, with a little black bristly moustache and two wandering eyebrows which went halfway to the stratosphere. Black hair was draped over his head like an old rug, with a pair of wire-rimmed glasses perched on top. But it was his eyes which really freaked me out. They were the palest pale blue you ever saw, fearsomely intense, and completely mad.

"We … " I tried to think desperately of an excuse.

" … are in my house," he completed.

I looked to Kevin for help, but Kevin was literally scared rigid. "We're on a project," I blurted. "A school project. About Dorothy Wordsearch."

At the mention of Dorothy Wordsearch, the strange man seemed to flinch slightly, then recover himself. "How long have you been here?" he barked. "What have you seen?"

"Nothing!" I blabbed.

The man looked from me to Kevin, then from Kevin to me. He seemed to be weighing us up in some way. "Well," he said, "I shall have to show you round, shan't I?" Suddenly he broke into a smile.

I think it was supposed to be a welcoming smile, but it only added to his look of complete madness.

"Now," he said. "Where shall we start?"

The strange man wandered back down the hall, stroking his chin thoughtfully. Not knowing what else to do, we followed.

"Well," he said. "You might as well see command HQ."

To my amazement, the man opened the door to the old study and ushered us inside.

Nothing could have prepared me for what was inside that study. The room was a shrine to Fluffy Bunny Button, with FBB posters, giant blow-up FBB dolls, FBB duvet covers, FBB sweatshirts, FBB backpacks, even an FBB portable stereo. Above it all was a map of Milton Keynes.

"Make yourself at home," said the man.

I squatted nervously on a Fluffy Bunny Button pouffe. Kevin knelt on a FBB rug.

The man beamed widely.

"So," he said. "Do you have questions?"

"Er … " I mumbled.

"You're doing a project," said the man. "So you must have questions."

"I've got a question," said Kevin.

I frowned at Kevin, as if to say "For goodness' sake, don't say anything stupid!"

"Fire away," said the man.

"Who are you?" asked Kevin.

I cringed. To my relief, however, the man didn't seem too bothered. "Who am I?" he replied. "Well, that is an easy question. I, young man, am Winston Wordsearch."

I was stunned. Winston Wordsearch? Dotty's late husband, the eccentric scientist, buried two years back?

"But you're dead!" blurted Kevin.

"Oh I am, am I?" replied the man. "And who told you that?"

"We read it," I gabbled, before Kevin

could make things worse. "On a website."

"Well," said Winston Wordsearch (if it really was him), "the website was obviously having you on."

I looked again at the strange, stretched skin on his face, the black rug on his head, the pale, pale eyes. He looked like something that had crawled out from under a stone ...

... or someone who'd been kept in a cellar for two years.

"Next question," he pronounced.

I looked around the room. "What is all this stuff?" I asked.

"This," replied Winston Wordsearch, "is the Future. A world where every child has heard of Fluffy Bunny Button, where every child wants a Fluffy Bunny doll, a Fluffy Bunny toothbrush, and a Fluffy Bunny hairbrush-and-makeup kit. These, of course, are merely prototypes. But when the Fluffy Bunny movie comes out, and the craze really takes hold, we will be ready to go into mass production. Can you imagine how rich that will make us?"

"Us?" I repeated.

"Me, and my wonderful wife, Dorothy," explained Winston Wordsearch.

The words "wonderful" and "Dorothy" somehow didn't quite go together in my mind.

"But she's dead too!" blurted Kevin.

"Who told you that?" rasped Winston.

"There was a funeral notice," I gabbled. "In the village."

Winston gave a little sad smile. "There is some truth in what you say," he announced.

"How can there be *some* truth in it?" asked Kevin. "She's either dead or she isn't."

"Not necessarily," replied Winston, an even madder glint in his eye. "Would you like to meet her?"

Chapter Seven

A chill breeze suddenly swept through the old house. A hundred bad memories fought for space in my head. No, I did not want to meet Dorothy Wordsearch – or whatever it was that looked so very much like her.

"Maybe later," I blurted. "We don't want to interrupt her work."

"She *is* working very hard at the moment," continued Winston. "We've just sent a book to the publishers. Dotty wasn't really ready to write it so soon, but unfortunately, we have a problem."

Winston leaned closer. His eyes became very fierce. "*Someone*," he said, "is trying to take over Fluffy Bunny Button."

"Never," I muttered.

"Two despicable jumped-up kids. They won some kind of prize, apparently, and it obviously went to their heads. They thought they could just muscle in and take over! They thought they could destroy my dream! Can you imagine how that makes me feel?"

Winston's hands closed on an imaginary throat, and throttled it very thoroughly.

I smiled nervously.

"What did you say your names were?" he barked.

I turned to Kevin. My brain had gone to mush. "What were our names?" I asked.

"I'm Hamish Cock-a-leekie," replied Kevin, "and you're Bunty Butterbean."

"Very unusual names," noted Winston, suspiciously.

"We're very unusual people," replied Kevin.

"But not as unusual as those two kids that wrote *The Ghost of the Chocolate Dinosaur*," I gabbled.

Winston's eyes narrowed. "Did I mention the name of the book they wrote?" he enquired.

"We did it in school," I blurted.

"Hmmm," said Winston, irritably. "Soon there will only be one book on the national curriculum, and that will be Fluffy Bunny Button."

"Heaven," I said.

"Fluffy bun-tastic," said Kevin.

"Indeed," replied Winston. He checked his watch. "Oh, it's her break time anyway," he said. "I may as well introduce you to her now."

"No!" I cried. "You can't!"

"Why is that?" asked Winston.

"Kevin's got nits!" I blurted.

"What?" said Kevin.

"Massive ones, like … hamsters!" I cried.

"No, I haven't!" snapped Kevin, who obviously hadn't caught on to my gameplan.

Winston gave me an odd look, then shook his head in a bewildered way. "I'll ring for her now," he pronounced.

Before we could utter another word, Winston pressed the nose of a Fluffy Bunny intercom. "Come down now, darling," he said. "Oh, and bring your work."

Within seconds we heard the CLUMP CLUMP CLUMP of heavy feet on the stairs, matched by the THUMP THUMP THUMP of my heart. Now we were surely done for. Whatever state she was in, Dotty was certain to recognize us.

The door swung open, and there she stood. Dorothy Wordsearch, the world's worst children's author, wearing a large violet tent and the same paisley shawl I had last seen hanging from Mr Collins's teeth.

"Come and meet Hamish and Bunty," said Winston.

Dorothy Wordsearch began to move forward, stiffly and in a dead straight line. She wore a mild, meaningless smile and her eyes stared at a spot just to the left of my head. It seemed to take her an age to register where we were, and when her dreaded eyes finally met mine, there was not a hint of recognition.

"I'm very pleased to meet you, Hamish," she pronounced, in a woolly monotone.

"That is Bunty, darling," Winston corrected her.

"I'm very pleased to meet you, Bunty Darling."

"And you," I muttered, nervously.

At this, Dorothy Wordsearch's smile broadened into the most sickly grin you could imagine. It was the false smile of a little child desperate to please.

Dotty greeted Kevin in the same way, then walked meekly up to Winston and handed him her work.

"That's a very good girl," said Winston.

"Thank you," replied Dotty, faintly.

"Hamish and Bunty are doing a project about you, dear," said Winston.

"A project," repeated Dotty, without seeming to understand very much.

"Yes, dear," said Winston. "A project. Now run along and make us a cup of tea."

"Yes, darling," replied Dotty. With that, she backed out of the room, bowing as she did so.

"A wonderful woman, my wife," mused Winston. "Now, let's see how she's done."

By now I didn't know what to think.

This was certainly not the Dotty I remembered – not one bit like her. I often imagined poor old Winston being her servant, but certainly not the other way around.

Winston nodded thoughtfully as he read his beloved wife's work. Suddenly, however, a look of confusion came over him, followed by a frown, which grew deeper and deeper the more he read.

"Oh no, no, no," he muttered. "This won't do at all!"

Winston put down the story and sighed.

"Those damn kids!" he exclaimed. "If it wasn't for them, she wouldn't have had to work so hard, and then *this* wouldn't have happened!"

"Is something the matter?" I asked.

"She's malfunctioning," replied Winston.

"Malfunctioning?" I repeated. It seemed an odd word to use, as well as a very long one.

"See for yourself," said Winston, handing me the story.

I began to read:

FLUFFY BUNNY BUTTON ALL AT SEA
A new story by Dorothy Wordsearch

Fluffy Bunny Button was more excited than ever. Today he was going down to Goldensand-on-sea, where his best friend Goody Bunny Twoshoes had a boat!

It was a lovely yellow motorboat, with a blue funnel and a brussel sprout mast!

Fluffy and Goody set sail beneath a beautiful hot purple sprouting sun. It wasn't long before they were in the middle of the cauliflower ocean.

"This is the royal jersey new potato life," said Fluffy Bunny Button.

I put down the story. "It's a bit weird, isn't it?" I commented.

"We've had this problem before," replied Winston. "When she's running down, she starts inserting random vegetables."

I made a good show of being concerned. "Can anything be done about it?" I asked.

"She'll have to be recharged," replied Winston.

Now the alarm bells really began to ring. "Recharged?" I repeated.

"I'd better explain," said Winston.

"A while ago," began Winston, playing absent-mindedly with a Fluffy Bunny paperweight, "my wife had an unfortunate accident. I won't go into the details, but the result of this accident was that Dorothy was, to all intents and purposes, dead. However, due to the miracles of modern science, clever people such as myself are able to create new life out of almost anything. In my wife's case, all I had was a fragment of DNA on an old shawl. However, with a little genetic engineering and a few bits and bobs, I was able to get Dorothy on the road again."

"She's a … clone?" I asked.

"Not exactly," replied Winston. "Part of her is human tissue, but there's a few nuts and bolts and silicon chips involved as well. In some ways, she's the same old Dorothy I've always known. In other ways she's a cyborg."

"That's why she does everything you say!" blurted Kevin.

"Well," replied Winston. "there wouldn't be much sense in making a wife who *didn't* do what I said, would there?"

I felt I should object in some way, but that mad look had come into

Winston's eyes again, and I thought it best to button my lip.

"Wouldn't *you* like a wife who did as she was told, Hamish?" asked Winston, with a matey wink.

"I'm not getting married!" snapped Kevin.

"Not even to your girlfriend here?" asked Winston.

I was horrified. "I'm not his girlfriend!" I howled.

"Ooh!" said Winston, wincing. "Such a shrill tongue! You don't want to be putting up with that, Hamish! Next thing she'll be taking over completely, and locking you in the cellar!"

Winston's face had suddenly become very angry. He quickly covered this with a smile and a laugh, but now I knew my hunch was right. Dotty had made a prisoner of her beloved husband, and now the tables were turned.

"Of course, the best thing about having a cyborg for a wife," continued Winston, "is that she doesn't give two hoots if you've got *another woman*!"

Winston gave a long, theatrical wink and punched Kevin playfully on the shoulder. "*Another woman*," he repeated, "like my gorgeous, gorgeous girlfriend Tamara."

Winston winked again, and Kevin grinned. Kevin was really starting to take to this revolting man. The two of them chuckled together as Dotty reappeared, with a tray containing four cups of tea, a sugar bowl and a cream jug.

"Oh no, dear," said Winston. "We won't be needing four cups. Tamara won't be back till later."

"Oh! I'm so sorry," replied Dotty.

"Run along now," said Winston.

Dotty meekly obeyed. The whole business was making me so sick, I almost wished the old Dotty would reappear.

"Now," said Winston, "how are you two at catching rabbits?"

"Catching rabbits?" I repeated.

"The fields round here are full of them," said Winston. "I'm sure you can bag one or two."

"Why have we got to catch rabbits?" I asked.

"Come with me," said Winston. "I'll show you out the back, and then everything will become clear."

Chapter Eight

So the time had come to revisit the Secret Garden. You cannot imagine my dread as Winston turned that huge old key in the back door lock. I could still imagine Mr Collins out there – that towering monster with the head of a giant insect, vicious piranha teeth, limp useless wings and savage grasping claws. I could still see him swaying so close I could smell his rancid breath, as he tugged against his shackles with unearthly groans.

We never knew what had happened to Mr Collins, of course. We saw him escape, but no one had sighted him since. Maybe he had been captured, or returned of his own accord. Or maybe Winston had replaced him with something even more hideous.

The door swung slowly open.

Outside there was a pleasant patio, with ornamental roses, tasteful garden furniture and a tinkling water feature.

Beyond that was a red cedarwood summer house, a perfect site for soaking up the sun on a long summer afternoon, with a glass of lemonade and a nice story about ponies.

"Welcome to the clinic," said Winston.

We approached the summer house. I noticed that the windows were made of frosted glass, the kind you get in toilets.

"This," said Winston, "is where my lovely wife recharges."

"Recharges?" I repeated.

"That's what I said," trilled Winston.

We went inside. It was like a wendy house crossed with a dentist's surgery, with one reclining chair on either side, something like an overgrown stereo in the middle, and a kind of small aquarium, minus the water, above this.

"This is where the rabbit goes," said Winston, indicating the aquarium thing.

"What do you do to it?" I asked, anxiously.

"Well, *basically*," explained Winston, "I suck out its brainwaves … and transfer them to Dorothy."

"Does it die?" I asked, horrified.

"Oh, no," replied Winston. "It just becomes a trifle—"

"A trifle?" trilled Kevin. "Wicked!"

"A trifle vacant, I was going to say," continued Winston.

Winston mimed a rabbit with an out-to-lunch expression. Kevin laughed.

"For good?" I asked, getting more alarmed by the second.

"Not to worry," replied Winston. "A rabbit isn't that bright in the first place."

Kevin laughed again, but I was looking round in dismay. "And why are there two chairs?" I asked.

"Well," replied Winston. "Sometimes Dorothy likes to sit on *this* side ... and sometimes Dorothy likes to sit on *that* side. It depends on how the sun hits the summer house."

I wasn't convinced. And I certainly didn't want to catch rabbits so Winston could suck their brains out.

"Thanks," I said, "but I think I'll go home now."

Winston turned to Kevin with an exasperated look on his face. "Women!" he complained.

Tut-tut-tut, went Kevin.

Winston drew a deep breath. "I hope

you're not going to disappoint me," he said. "For some time now, I've been thinking about getting a couple of bright young kids to help out. It's all getting a bit much for me, you see. I'm too old to catch rabbits, for a start. And I can't always rely on Tamara. You two came along just at the right time."

I did not look enthusiastic. Winston decided to ignore me and focus all his attention on Kevin. "Let me show you just how much fun you could be having, Kevin," he said.

We went back inside the house. Dorothy was busy in the kitchen, washing up the cups of tea we hadn't drunk.

"There's a good girl," said Winston. "And when you've finished, I want you to go back to your desk, and take all the vegetables out of your story."

"I'll be as fast as I can," replied Dotty, timidly.

"You've missed a bit here," said Kevin, picking up a cup. He winked at Winston, who gave him a playful dig in the ribs.

"And now," declared Winston, "it's playtime!"

Winston made his way to the room beneath the stairs, Miss Birdshot's old room, the one with the metal grille. Kevin followed, swaggering like a Western gunslinger. Winston unlocked the grille, then heaved it up, to reveal the most unexpected thing. It was a beautiful shiny blue dodgem car, styled like a space rocket, with fat black bumpers and a pole reaching up to the wire mesh ceiling – the ceiling that seemed so familiar earlier.

"That's ba-a-a-d!" enthused Kevin, eyes popping.

"Now you will see what life is for!" said Winston.

Winston invited Kevin into the passenger seat, then threw a big switch marked JUICE, climbed behind the wheel, and pressed the power pedal to the floor. The space-age dodgem shot forward, almost crushing me against the wall, then set off on a mad higgledy-piggledy charge down the hall, bouncing off the walls like a pinball. Kevin jerked and juddered in his seat, face full of unspeakable glee, while Winston's eyes were fixed before him with a terrifying manic gleam.

The dodgem disappeared into the old classroom, from which came the sounds of thumps and bumps and devilish laughter. Back out they shot, with Winston swinging the wheel like a jiving dancer, and Kevin looking like one of those born-again religious people who had just seen the light. After a few more madcap circuits they finally came to rest about two millimetres from my fragile toes.

Winston climbed out, beaming fiercely. "Your turn now, Kevin!" he said.

"And Jasmin can be pass—"

Too late. Kevin was gone. Off like a cannonball, smashing head-first into the wall, then careering away like a drunken nuclear-powered bluebottle. Teachers in our school would not trust Kevin with a roller skate. The thought of him in a powered vehicle would probably turn them into nervous wrecks.

When he finally stopped, at least ten minutes later, Kevin's eyes were even madder than Winston's. "Wicked!" he yelled. "What's next?"

"Next," said Winston, "we hunt rabbits!"

Chapter Nine

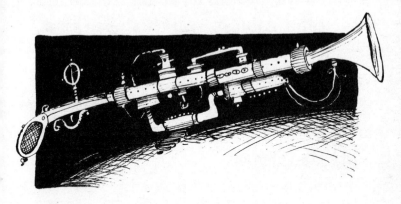

At the rear of the summer house was a
river. It was a wide, fast river, with a narrow
iron bridge across it. On the other side of
this bridge were the fields. That was where
the rabbits lived, hopping and nibbling
and burrowing, pitifully ignorant that
Kevin was stomping towards them with a
sonic stunner in his hands.

I had never heard of a sonic stunner,
but that was probably because Winston
had only just invented it. The sonic
stunner looked a bit like a hockey stick
with a trigger. When you pulled the trigger

it sent a concentrated high-frequency sound wave towards its target. The sound wave could confuse a human being for a second, or knock out a rabbit for a minute. Winston said we had to find a rabbit that was not too far away, stun it, then run over and stuff it in a nice carry-box which he had also designed.

Kevin was up for this in a big way. He began to race across the fields in a crazy zigzag, aiming at anything that moved. I trudged behind, lugging the carry-box.

"Seen one!" he screamed, raising the sonic stunner.

"Wait!" I yelled. "It's no good stunning it if you haven't got the box!"

Kevin stamped his feet in frustration. "We've *lost* it!" he shrieked.

I finally caught up. "Shame," I said.

"You're not trying!" he bawled.

"You're right," I replied.

"I'll do it all myself!" cried Kevin, grabbing at the box.

I held tight. "Kevin!" I hissed. "Just *think* for a moment!"

"What now?" he snapped.

I put down the box and sat on it, inviting Kevin to do the same. Kevin preferred to stay hopping from one foot to the other.

"Listen, Kevin," I said. "We came here to stop them writing books, not help them!"

"No we never," said Kevin. "We came here to find out what was going on, and now we've found out, and it's great!"

"It's evil!" I cried. "Sucking out a rabbit's brains just to write a stupid children's book!"

"You write stupid children's books!" snapped Kevin. "You wrote *Fluffy Bunny Button's Brand New Bike*, and you cut out

Maggoty May without asking me!"

"You're not still on about that!" I cried.

"Just cos Winston likes me and not you," mumbled Kevin.

"I don't want Winston to like me!" I snapped. "He's a creepy old man and if you trust him, you're an idiot!"

"Tell you what," said Kevin. "You go home, and I'll just have a really good time on my own."

"I will," I replied.

"Good," said Kevin.

"Bye then," I replied.

With that I set off across the fields. I didn't know which way I was heading, but I didn't really care. Obviously there was *some* way to get away from this place, and it was just a matter of finding it.

And then I arrived at the river again.

Try another way, I thought.

I stomped off in another direction.

After a few hundred yards I arrived at … the river.

Try again, I thought. Another hundred yards and … you guessed it.

The whole area was encircled.

As far as I knew, rivers did not normally go round in circles, but with Winston around, anything was possible. Maybe it had been cut out, like a canal, or given some pills to make it turn corners. Whatever the reason, there was no escape.

Suddenly I heard an excited cry. "Ye-e-e-e-es!"

Kevin was leaping up and down like a demented frog. A shiver of alarm went through me as I realized he had bagged a rabbit. As he picked up the carry-box and began lugging it across the field, I set off towards the place he was heading. Kevin saw me and picked up his pace. I picked up my pace. Kevin began to run. I began

to run. Kevin ran faster. I sprinted like a greyhound. The rabbit came into sight, lying on its side, completely still. I had to get there before Kevin could stuff it in the box … and I did, just. I dived full-length and got both hands round the rabbit's middle. It felt very warm, and soft, and fragile.

"You give me that rabbit!" cried Kevin, panting.

"No!" I cried. "Leave it!"

Kevin dropped the box and grabbed the other end of the rabbit. Now I was in a hopeless position. I couldn't let the rabbit be used for a tug-of-war. If Kevin pulled, I'd have to let go – which is exactly what happened. As I cursed and screamed, he fed the rabbit into the carry-box.

"It's *my* rabbit!" he cried. "Aren't you, Fluffy Bunny Brain-dead?"

"Let it go!" I yelled. "And don't call it that!"

"Well, don't call me Kevin!" answered Kevin. "Cos my name is Hamish!"

With that, Kevin started trudging back towards the house with his prize. He'd always been a nutter, but I'd never seen him lose it as badly as this. The thought of another dodgem ride had completely turned his head. Nothing I could say would make a blind bit of difference.

Winston, needless to say, was most delighted with Kevin's work.

"An excellent specimen," he said, viewing the rabbit as it hopped frantically around its box.

"Best one I saw," replied Kevin, beaming.

"Brain is small, of course," said Winston, "but it should keep the wife going for a day or two."

"I could catch a cow if you like," said Kevin.

"No, I prefer a rabbit," replied Winston.

The rabbit ran its scuttery paws up the side of the cage, nose twitching. By now I was hopelessly in love with it.

"Right," said Winston. "Let's get to work."

"No!" I yelped.

"Pardon?" said Winston.

"It's too soon," I gabbled. "Tamara's not back." This was the first thing that came into my head, but luckily enough, it did make Winston pause for thought.

"Tamara does like to see the recharges," said Winston.

"Yes," I gabbled. "And you could maybe have a cup of tea first, and I could look after the rabbit—"

"Get lost, Jasmin!" blurted Kevin.

Winston stopped short. "Jasmin?" he said. "I thought you said her name was Bunty."

Kevin's face dropped as he realized his

dreadful mistake. "It is," he stammered. "I call her Jasmin to annoy her, cos she's yellow."

Winston frowned. "I don't like that name," he said. "It's the name of *that girl*. The one who tried to steal Fluffy Bunny Button."

"Is it?" peeped Kevin.

Winston viewed me clinically, as if I were a specimen in a jar. His hand squeezed hard on the pen he was holding, and there was a sharp CRACK. "You've reminded me why we've no time to lose," he said. "Tamara will just have to miss this show."

Dotty was summoned. She came down clutching another pile of papers, which she offered hopefully to Winston.

"I *think* I've got it right this time, darling," she said.

I glanced over Winston's shoulder:

Runner Bean Runner Bean Runner Bean
By Dorothy Runner Bean

Runner bean runner bean runner bean. Runner bean runner bean runner bean.

"Runner bean runner bean runner bean runner bean?" runner bean. Runner bean runner bean runner bean!

"OK, Dorothy," said Winston, "You'd better come with me."

Chapter Ten

It was a lovely golden evening in Dotty W.'s summer house. Dotty sat in her favourite chair with a bright shiny helmet on her head. Nearby, Fluffy Bunny Brain-dead hopped around in his new glass box. Fluffy Bunny Brain-dead had a little helmet too, a special one with holes for his ears and a long curly wire leading off to a perfectly splendid machine.

Winston W. stood by this machine looking very proud of himself.

"It's not easy making all this stuff, you know," he proclaimed. "The nearest hardware shop is over five miles away, and they hardly ever have wingnuts."

"Can I pull the lever?" asked Kevin, who, as usual, wasn't listening.

"I rather think Bunty should have that honour," replied Winston, fixing me with his sinister smile. "What do you say, Bunty?"

"I think it's mad," I blurted.

"Mad?" repeated Winston. "How is that?"

"What if she gets too much power?" I gabbled. "She might take over again! She might … lock you in the cellar again!"

There. I'd said it. I feared Winston would go into a rage, but he simply gave a sad chuckle. When he spoke again, it was in a hushed, serious tone.

"Who told you she locked me in the cellar?" he asked.

"You did," I blurted. "When you were drunk … in the dodgem, with Tamara."

"I did?" asked Winston, doubtfully.

"We overheard," I said, and shot a threatening look to Kevin, as if to say Just Shut Up. Winston hung his head and for a while seemed lost in thought. But when his head came back up, he was smiling brightly.

"Nice try, Bunty," he said. "I know you want to save the little bunny. But I've dealt with what Dorothy did to me. And the fact is, she will never control me again. I cut that side of her out of her genes. I suppose you could say it is my revenge. Isn't it, dear? Isn't it, you sad, pathetic old bat?"

"Yes, darling," replied Dotty, with a gentle smile.

"A wonderful woman, my wife," said Winston. "Now, enough of these delays. It's showtime!"

I gazed in horror as Winston seized the lever. Then, from nowhere, came a tiny tinny version of *The Wheels on the Bus Go Round and Round*.

It was Winston's mobile phone.

"Yes?" he snapped, angrily. Then his eyes softened. "Tamara!" he purred. "We're in the summer house!"

Winston put down the phone. His face was filled with an almost childish glee. "Tamara's back!" he beamed. His hand relaxed on the lever as he awaited the mysterious woman who was his girlfriend.

The back door of the house slammed shut. Clattery footsteps pattered swiftly across the patio. All eyes went to the door of the summer house. Creakily it opened, and there, to my horror, stood the unmistakable figure of Dotty's old housekeeper, Miss Birdshot.

However, like Dotty, Miss Birdshot had undergone some remarkable changes. The skin on her face was all stretched, like Winston's, and in place of her old dustcoat she wore a ridiculous leather skirt and leopard-print blouse. On her old feet were pointed lace-up ankle boots, and perched at an angle on her head was a raspberry beret.

"Lammikins!" she croaked.

"Pet possum!" purred Winston.

"Miss … Miss … Broccoli!" blubbered Dotty.

Miss Birdshot was not interested in her old mistress. She was blind to the existence of anyone except her boyfriend. They embraced in the most disgusting way, which I won't describe too closely, except to say there was a lot of slobbering.

"It's all set up to go, possum," said Winston, indicating his brilliant machine.

"All in working order?" snapped Miss Birdshot.

"We were just about to find out," replied Winston.

"'We'?" repeated Miss Birdshot. For the first time she cast her eyes about her, and saw the two of us shrinking into the corner.

Would she remember us? Had her brain been changed as much as her face?

I soon got my answer, as a frown like thunder settled on to her brows.

"What are *they* doing here?" she railed.

"This is Bunty and Hamish," replied Winston. "My new apprentices."

"What?" yelled Miss Birdshot. "But I know these children!"

Now the game really was up.

"Run, Kevin!" I yelled, but Miss Birdshot was as quick as ever. The door slammed shut and the tiny but powerful old woman blocked any hope of escape.

"Tamara!" cried Winston. "What on earth is going on?"

Miss Birdshot levelled a scaly claw at my face. "She's the one!" she cawed. "She's the one who stole Fluffy Bunny Button!"

Winston's face hardened. It seemed to be just what he wanted to hear. "I knew it," he hissed.

Now the old housekeeper turned to Kevin. "And this," she rasped, "is her partner in crime!"

Winston's face fell. "Not Hamish!" he cried.

"His name is not Hamish!" barked Miss Birdshot. "His name is Kevin *Shilling*." Miss Birdshot spat this last word out in such a shrill tone that all the windows shook.

Winston put a hand to his head and went into another silence. When he spoke again, it was in a soft, dreadful voice. "Oh, Hamish," he said. "You have let me down badly."

"We just wanted … to keep Fluffy Bunny Button alive," peeped Kevin.

"Is that so," replied Winston, without feeling. Then a thought struck him, and he broke into the most sinister smile of the day. "Well," he said, "as you both care so much about rabbits, I think we should let this one go."

With that, Winston went to the glass box, removed the helmet from the rabbit, took the rabbit to the door, and opened it. The rabbit didn't need any encouragement. It disappeared like a shot, leaving me wondering what next?

I soon found out.

"As I said earlier," said Winston, "a rabbit's brain will only keep Dorothy going for a few days. A *human* brain, on the other hand …"

My knees went weak. I knew there was a reason for the second chair!

"Seize the boy!" barked Winston.

In an instant, Miss Birdshot's vice-like hands clamped round Kevin's arms. She had lost nothing of her fantastic strength. I flailed hopelessly with butterfly fists, but Miss Birdshot barely felt them. Before Kevin knew what had hit him, he was in the chair, with a helmet on his head and Fluffy Bunny Button handkerchiefs tied round his arms and legs.

"Not me!" he cried. "I'm an idiot! You don't want my brain!"

"But Hamish," replied Winston, "you have already proved how intelligent you are. It was you who caught the rabbit, after all."

Winston took hold of the lever once more. Miss Birdshot pinned me to the wall and stifled my yells with her scaly vulture's claw. Kevin's eyes opened wide in horror as Winston brought his full force down, down on the lever. The machine clacked and hummed into life. The transfer had begun. Soon, Dotty would be full of frenzied creative energy and Kevin would be ... a vegetable.

After a few seconds, however, it was clear something was wrong.

"This can't be right," muttered Winston. "I'm getting double the normal readings for this boy's brain waves!"

"Is it within the safety limits?" asked Miss Birdshot.

"Only just," replied Winston. "If his head gets any more active, I don't know what will happen."

Immediately something clicked in my own brain – an idea, just as bright as any of Kevin's. I felt in my pocket, and sure enough, there was a crackly packet in there – a packet containing the rest of the cherry jelly rings.

This, I thought, could be our last chance.

With a sudden urgent wriggle I broke free of Miss Birdshot's grasp and dashed towards the machine. "Kevin!" I cried. "Quick! Eat these!"

With fumbling fingers, I crammed every last cherry jelly ring into Kevin's mouth. Miss Birdshot leapt upon me like a tigress, but my work was already done. Kevin chomped furiously, eyes spinning, fingernails tapping. Alarm spread across Winston's face.

"The waves!" he cried. "They're out of control!"

Over in the other chair, a thin wisp of blue smoke was coming out of Dotty's ears. Kevin chewed and swallowed, chewed and swallowed, like some crazy combine harvester.

"She's going to blow!" cried Winston. He dived for cover, pulling Miss Birdshot with him, and setting me free. Suddenly there was an enormous retching noise, like everyone in the world throwing up at the same time. Dotty, Kevin and the entire machine disappeared behind a cloud of brown smoke, and when it finally cleared, Dotty was as dumb as a ventriloquist's dummy and Kevin was standing next to me, rubbing his head.

"Can we go now?" he said. "I've got a headache."

Chapter Eleven

It was a long, long journey home, partly because we had to walk to the station, and partly because Kevin did not shut up for at least two hours. I began to wonder if I'd done the right thing to save him. Then, suddenly, he shut up, looked around himself, realized he was on a train, and for the first time, noticed I was there.

"Where are we going?" he asked.

"What do you mean, where are we going?" I replied. "We're going home, of course!"

"Oh," said Kevin. "Where have we been?"

"Are you trying to be funny?" I asked.

Kevin looked blank. If he was trying to be funny, he was keeping a very straight face about it. I began recalling our many adventures at the old school: the meeting with Winston, the cyborg Dotty, catching the rabbit, the brain-sucking machine and the new Miss Birdshot, and finally, my heroic act of flinging the cherry jelly rings. Kevin greeted them all with the same twisted-face look of disbelief.

"You really remember nothing?" I asked.

"Last thing I remember is being in your shed," replied Kevin.

Kevin really did seem to mean it. On the other hand, it was very convenient for him to forget how Winston had taken him in, what a selfish toad he'd been, and the fact that I had saved the day. Still, I made sure he did hear about these things, some of them several times over.

Kevin seemed genuinely shocked at own behaviour. He didn't actually say sorry, but he did look a bit sorry, as well as baffled.

"But why did we go back to that place?" he asked.

I explained about the mysterious new adventure of Fluffy Bunny Button, and how this had threatened our new writing career.

"You mean *we* were writing Fluffy Bunny Button books?" asked Kevin.

"That's right," I replied.

"*Why?*" gasped Kevin.

"Well … they asked us," I replied.

Kevin shook his head. "I wouldn't have written that rubbish," he sniffed, "not if you paid me."

"Kevin," I replied. "You *were* being paid. A lot of money."

"Hah!" snorted Kevin. "I can't be bought!"

Kevin folded his arms very dramatically, as if to put a full stop on the conversation. If only I'd had a video, showing us fighting over that rabbit which he'd been so keen to sacrifice for Fluffy Bunny Button.

There was no point in arguing about it now. At least I had the satisfaction of knowing that, when it came down to it, it was me that couldn't be bought. "When I get back," I thought to myself, "I'll make myself a badge saying CAN'T BE BOUGHT, and wear it everywhere."

"What are you going to do when you get back, Kev?" I asked, following this line of thought.

"What do you think?" replied Kevin.

"I don't know," I said.

"I'm going down Whitesands Fun Park," declared Kevin, "and I'm going crazy hyper mental in them dodgems!"